fairy tales
for grown-ups

JENNIFER ROWE
fairy tales

for grown-ups

ALLEN&UNWIN

This edition published in 2001
First published in 2000 as *Angela's Mandrake and Other Feisty Fables*

Copyright © Jennifer Rowe 2000

All rights reserved. No part of this book may be reproduced or transmitted in any form or by any means, electronic or mechanical, including photocopying, recording or by any information storage and retrieval system, without prior permission in writing from the publisher. The *Australian Copyright Act* 1968 (the Act) allows a maximum of one chapter or 10 per cent of this book, whichever is the greater, to be photocopied by any educational institution for its educational purposes provided that the educational institution (or body that administers it) has given a remuneration notice to Copyright Agency Limited (CAL) under the Act.

Allen & Unwin
83 Alexander Street,
Crows Nest NSW 2065 Australia
Phone: (61 2) 8425 0100
Fax: (61 2) 9906 2218
E-mail: info@allenandunwin.com
Web: www.allenandunwin.com

National Library of Australia
Cataloguing-in-Publication entry:

Rowe, Jennifer, 1948– .
 Fairy tales for grown-ups.

 ISBN 1 86508 642 8.

 1. Mandrakes—Fiction. 2. Fairy tales. I. Title.

A823.4

Design and illustrations by Donna Rawlins, Monkeyfish
Set in 13/18pt Bembo by DOCUPRO, Sydney
Printed in Australia by McPherson's Printing Group

10 9 8 7 6 5 4 3

Contents

The Magic Fish	1
The Lonely Prince	8
Curly Locks	17
Dr Knight and the Dragon	37
The Fat Wife	46
Justin and the Troll	63
Angela's Mandrake	79

For Mim and Van—true believers in the magic of love, humour and happy endings.

The Magic Fish

One day, a woman of middle years was wandering alone by the fish tank in her dentist's waiting room. As she wandered, she wept. She felt very sad and afraid, because she knew that her fondness for chocolate and those little round green and white things with chewy mint in the middle had damaged her teeth considerably.

'Why do you weep?' said a small, bubbly voice.

The woman was startled, for she had thought she was alone. The prim young receptionist had gone out for lunch, and there were no other patients waiting.

'Here!' said the voice.

To her surprise, the woman realised that a small gold fish was staring at her from the tank and that it was this that had spoken.

She put her nose quite close to the glass, to be sure.

'Why do you weep?' the fish asked again.

'I weep because my teeth ache, and so does my heart,' said the woman of middle years. 'I have led a life of dental wickedness. I have feasted on chocolate and those little round green and white things with chewy mint in the middle. I have not flossed regularly. I have broken many appointments, and torn up many reminder notices. Now I am ashamed and afraid. The dentist will be angry with me, and will make me pay for my sins in more ways than one. And the dental nurse, who is the daughter of an old school acquaintance, will see my shame.'

'If you set me free, I will grant you three wishes,' said the fish.

The woman rubbed the mist of her breath from the glass with one sleeve, and the tears from her eyes with the other. She could hardly believe her good fortune.

'What is your first wish?' asked the fish.

The woman opened her mouth to ask for perfect teeth, the teeth she'd had when she was a lithe young girl who thought she was immortal. Then her conscience pricked her, for she was not wicked through and through—only when it came to dental hygiene.

'I wish for world peace,' she said.

'Very well,' said the fish. 'No sooner said than done. What is your second wish?'

The woman thought of her family and friends, whom she loved dearly and who loved her despite her many fillings and extensive root canal therapy.

'I wish for long and happy lives for my family and friends,' she said.

'Certainly,' said the fish. It paused. 'You meant the phrase "my family" to include you yourself, I imagine?' it added.

'Oh, yes,' the woman replied hastily, crossing her fingers.

'What is your third wish?' asked the fish. 'And, remember, this is the last.'

The woman of middle years thought very, very carefully. She thought of famine and drought and the environment. She thought of the ozone layer and cures for cancer and the political situation in various oppressed nations. Then she glanced at the closed door of the dentist's surgery and thought . . . I will only have one shot at this.

'I wish for perfect teeth,' she said. 'The teeth I had when I was a lithe young girl who thought she was immortal.'

'Excellent choice,' said the fish briskly. 'Considering the circumstances. Now, it is time for you to fulfil your part of the bargain.' It swam up to the top of the fish tank and waited, waving its tail impatiently.

The woman cupped her hand and lifted the fish out of the tank. Some water came with it, but soon that began to drip away through her fingers and soak into the carpet. The fish wriggled, and began to look a little uncomfortable.

'What happens now?' it asked.

But the woman did not know. She had thought the fish would. After all, it was the magic one.

The fish began to gasp and its eyes bulged.

The door to the surgery opened and a man of middle years hurried out, looking pale and ashamed. He darted a quick look at the woman and noted the dying fish in her hand. His smile would have been pleasant except that it was lopsided, and dribbling slightly from one corner.

'Just put it back,' he hissed, glancing over his shoulder.

Startled, the woman obeyed. The gold fish hit the water and plunged quickly down, taking great, relieved gasps. Then it retreated to the bottom of the tank and skulked in some weed, waving its fins in a huffy sort of way.

'No memory,' slurred the man of middle years. 'That's the trouble with fish. Even the magic ones. What did you wish for?'

'World peace, and so on,' said the woman, who wanted him to think well of her.

'Me too,' said the man, who wanted her to think well of him. 'But the deal is, the wishes don't come true till you've actually done the freeing bit. And you only get one shot at it.' Thoughtfully, he ran his fingers over his receding hairline. 'Shame about that,' he muttered.

They stood in silence for a moment, watching the fish. After a while, it started swimming around the tank again, staring at them curiously. Clearly, it had already forgotten the whole affair.

'So it won't be happening, then?' said the woman, to be sure. 'World peace, and—so on?'

The man shook his head sadly, and again he smoothed his hair. She felt strangely drawn to him.

Just then the prim young receptionist came back, sat behind her desk and looked enquiringly at the man, who pulled out his wallet.

At the same moment the dentist opened the door of his surgery. Through the door the woman of middle years could see the chair, and the instruments, and the dental nurse waiting with a paper bib. Her heart sank.

'I'll wait for you,' said the man, handing a credit card to the receptionist with a flourish. 'We could have a coffee—if you feel like it.'

'I probably won't,' said the woman, imagining herself drooling coffee down her front while he watched. Then she thought . . . I will only have one shot at this. 'But wait anyway—if you feel like it,' she added quickly.

He nodded, and grinned lopsidedly, giving another credit card to the receptionist because the first one hadn't worked.

The woman went into the surgery to meet her fate. What followed was not pleasant, but somehow easier than usual to bear. And when it was over, she and the man went out together into the golden afternoon and walked for hours, talking of many things, including their dental work, their children, their divorces (two, in his case), their hopes and fears, and magic.

As the sun set, they kissed. This was very nice, since by now they could both feel their lips again. Then they felt like celebrating, because, although world peace was still as far away as ever, a deep and certain peace was growing in their hearts.

So they had dinner. Fish and chips seemed appropriate. With chocolate mousse to follow.

The Lonely Prince

Once upon a time there was a kind and relatively handsome young man called Joel. As well as being kind and relatively handsome, with a good sense of humour, Joel had everything money could buy, for his father, Rex King, was the owner of King's Famous Fritzburger fast-food chain, and fabulously wealthy.

At the time this story begins, three beautiful, charming young women were vying for Joel's hand in marriage. But though he longed to find a partner in life, Joel could not bring himself to commit to any one of them. He enjoyed their company, but he felt no magic when they looked at him or breathed his name. He felt no longing to hold them close, or to give them all he had. He knew that this meant he was not in love.

He told himself that this was because he feared deception and betrayal. For as well being kind and relatively handsome, Joel was sensitive. He was haunted by the fear that the young women did not love him for himself alone, but for his father's money.

'So what?' said his father, who was not kind, handsome or sensitive at all. He himself had been widowed when Joel was just a child, and was fond of claiming that he was married to his business. When he needed female companionship he paid for it at the Bon-Bon Massage Parlour (Bouncy Babes, Discretion Assured) or, if the occasion was formal, the Top-Hole Escort Agency.

But Joel grew quieter and sadder by the day, and eventually his father became impatient.

'You're lucky to have a choice, boy,' he said. 'It's more than I had when I was your age. Just pick one of the three girls and marry her, for God's sake. You'll get fond of whoever it is, once you're settled. You're a softie, like your mother.'

Joel shook his head. 'How can I give my heart unless I'm sure that I'm loved for myself, not for your money?' he asked sadly.

Such talk made his father queasy, particularly over breakfast, but he persisted.

'Tell you what,' he said. 'How about you give them a product integrity test. Invite each one of them to dinner. But instead of taking them out, get them to meet you in a cheap motel. Instead of champagne and smoked trout, give them rough wine and take-away pizza. Tell them you and I have had a fight, and I've thrown you out, and you're broke. If they say they love you after that, you'll know they really love you for yourself. As if it matters.'

Reluctantly, Joel agreed to do as his father suggested. He booked three nights at the Kosy Kabins motel. He rang the three young women and made the appointments. He looked up a take-away pizza establishment in the phone book. He laid in a supply of cheap wine, both red and white.

On Friday night he entertained Sonia, the first of the girls on his list. Sonia was a top model. She was sultry and very beautiful—tall and slender as a reed, with skin like milk chocolate, lustrous black hair and eyes that seemed to burn like dark fire. She had always seemed very attracted to Joel, who had accompanied her to many charity balls.

But the motel room seemed not to suit her. She brooded on the lumpy couch like an eagle on a bread box. And when, after the pizza delivery man had come and gone, Joel told her how his father had thrown him out, she gave him a burning look and soon afterwards stalked out, saying that she had an early call.

Joel ate the pizza by himself, and drank the wine. He found he was in a strange state of excitement, but he could not think why.

On Saturday night, he had dinner with Louise, the second on his list. Louise was an actor. She had starred in several films and was presently the darling of a long-running TV series in which she played a madcap heart surgeon. She was small, perfumed and delicate, with a cloud of golden hair, blue eyes and dimples. She had always seemed very attracted to Joel, who had accompanied her to many premieres.

She nestled on the lumpy couch like a kitten, giggling that it was fun to rough it, and that it would be so refreshing to have a simple meal for a change. She flirted with the pizza delivery man, drank several glasses of wine, and sucked her fingers in a suggestive manner.

But when Joel told her how his father had thrown him out, she expressed sympathy in a melting voice, pressed her hand to her forehead, said that the wine had given her a headache and left, rather quickly.

Joel tossed and turned for most of the night. When he finally slept, he had strange, disturbing dreams. He woke with the dawn and lay very still, his heart racing and his palms sweating. He could hardly wait until the evening.

Sunday night's guest was Samantha, who owned her own PR agency and had not long ago been Young Businesswoman of the Year. She had a smooth cap of dark red hair, high cheekbones, clear green eyes, a wide, hard mouth and a dry wit. She had always seemed very attracted to Joel, who had accompanied her to many high-profile launches.

She sat on the arm of the lumpy couch and told Joel that the wine was revolting and that pizza was poison. When Joel told her that he was penniless, she laughed and offered to take *him* out to dinner. But by then the pizza delivery man had arrived, bringing free garlic bread because Joel had ordered three times in a week, and Joel said it would be wasteful not to eat it. So Samantha shook her head, put on her coat and left.

That night, Joel slept like a baby.

On Monday morning, he was home in time for breakfast.

'You look pleased with yourself,' his father said. 'Does that mean you've finally made up your mind?'

'More than that, Dad,' said Joel, toying dreamily with his muesli. 'I've fallen in love. At last.'

'So which one is it?' asked his father, who, though he cared little for his son, had become quite interested in the experiment.

'None of them,' said Joel. And he told his father, at some length, of his passion for Rodney, the pizza delivery man.

Rex King, who was as short on tolerance as he was on looks and espoused political correctness only in his advertisements, was furious and disgusted. He told his son to forget Rodney or get out.

Naturally, Joel chose the latter course. He packed a small bag and went to live with his new lover in a one-bedroom flat over a flower shop.

When Sonia heard the news she smouldered for two days and two nights. Not that anyone could tell the difference. When Samantha heard the news she laughed and rang all her friends. But when Louise heard the news she went straight round to see Rex King, to offer her condolences.

Rex was not deceived by her wide-eyed concern for

his feelings, but was very taken by her kittenish ways. In three months he had married her. He knew that she would cost him a good deal more, in the long term, than the Bon-Bon Massage Parlour but, as he told himself, at least he wouldn't have to go out for it. And, being a spiteful sort of girl, Louise would be the ideal person to gloat with over his pervert son's poverty.

Joel and Rodney lived on in the little flat over The Daisy Chain. Joel found part-time work wrapping chocolates for a small local firm. They were indeed poor, but they were very happy, and the free pizza Rodney received most nights kept the wolf from the door. Though his cholesterol count rose substantially, Joel did not regret his choice for a single moment.

Then, at the end of a full year, Rodney nervously confessed his secret. He was actually the heir to the massive Primrose Pickles fortune. He had taken a job as a pizza delivery man only to meet someone who loved him for himself alone.

Joel was very surprised, but of course he understood

Rodney's position only too well. He agreed with Rodney that they could be just as happy rich as they had been poor. So the very next day they gave up their jobs, moved into Rodney's beach-front mansion and bought two Dalmatians.

The news put Sonia in such an ill temper that her cover photograph for *Bogus* magazine became a legend. Samantha laughed, bitterly, and got drunk. Louise and Rex King spat chips.

But Joel and Rodney walked on the beach, played music, ate pizza only once a year, on their anniversary, and lived happily ever after.

Curly Locks

Once there was a young woman whose name was Annabel Smudge. She was small and slightly untidy-looking with gentle, widely spaced hazel eyes, curly, mouse-brown hair and a sweet, hesitating voice. She was not exactly simple, but she was not what most people would call a bright spark, either. Six days a week she worked as a cleaner in a factory that made staples, paperclips and metal edges for hanging files. Monday to Thursday evenings, after cooking dinner for her live-in boyfriend, Lawrence, who was an out-of-work security guard in delicate health, she would hurry to her local shopping centre to wash dishes at Tony's Good Eats, the cafe beside Pompey's Family Hair Salon.

Most people would have said that Annabel was in every way unremarkable. Even Lawrence thought so, though he was quite fond of her in his fashion, and she was useful to him. But in her childhood, as Annabel well remembered, things had been different.

Her mother and father had adored her. In those days her hair was golden, and her father had always called her Curly Locks. At night, on his return from the fishfingers factory, he would bounce her on his knee and chant:

> *Curly Locks, Curly Locks, wilt thou be mine?*
> *Thou shalt not wash dishes, nor yet feed the swine,*
> *But sit on a cushion and sew a fine seam,*
> *And feed upon strawberries, sugar and cream.*

'What's a swine, Daddy?' little Annabel would ask. And her father would sigh and stroke her curly head and say that he feared she would find out all too soon, bless her simple heart, and ignorance was bliss. Annabel didn't know what on earth he meant, but he never would explain.

When Annabel was seventeen, a bare year after her father had been retrenched from the factory, her parents achieved brief public notice by opening a letter bomb intended for a man whose name was also Smudge, but who lived somewhere else entirely. They died, Annabel liked to think, not horribly or in fear, but filled with the mild surprise that had always characterised their attitude to the unusual in life.

With their deaths, Annabel was left penniless and quite alone in the world. She was already working at the staple factory, and now she took on the dishwashing work as well, to pay back her parents' debts to the credit card company, the landlord and the chemist. She had been told she didn't have to do this, but she thought it was only right.

She met Lawrence soon afterwards, and fell in love with him at once. Unfortunately, his moving in with her, though it brought her great joy, didn't improve her financial situation. Lawrence turned out to be in such poor health that he could do little except lie on the couch all day watching television. Annabel was filled with love and sympathy for him, but sometimes, after coming home at midnight from her dishwashing job, she was so tired that she could barely drag herself around to do the housework. At these times she often thought of the rhyme her father used to sing to her, and she would laugh to herself. But not bitterly, for this wasn't in her nature. And not loudly, for she didn't want to disturb Lawrence, who by this time was tucked up in bed and sleeping surprisingly soundly for one so physically tormented.

Then, one hot, sultry Friday evening, everything changed.

Annabel was hurrying from the factory, intent on reaching home before the fishfingers she'd bought for dinner defrosted. She was on foot, for the traffic was heavy and the buses packed. She was only five minutes from the station when she turned a corner and found her way blocked by a row of mounted police. A demonstration against heavy traffic was in progress. Hundreds of determined-looking people with placards were sitting shoulder to shoulder on the road singing 'We Shall Overcome' as a round, with guitar accompaniment. Fights were breaking out everywhere as angry commuters struggled to pass through their ranks and besieged workers in surrounding buildings poured the dregs of coffee and chicken noodle soup from their windows.

Prudently unwilling to enter the fray, and very aware that her fishfingers grew limper with every moment she delayed, Annabel turned and hurried into a nearby men's clothing store that bore a sign saying 'Thru to Parkin Street. No One Asked to Buy'.

The store was large and very brightly lit. A maze of narrow paths threaded through tables piled high with flannelette shirts and underwear, and racks of identical suits behind which numbers of narrow-faced young salesmen lurked. Enormous signs advertising sale items hung on fishing line from the ceiling, slowly revolving as wheezing overhead fans stirred the thick air.

Clutching her shopping bag, Annabel sidled through the

maze, starting and mumbling as the young men approached her one by one, murmuring suggestively of suits, shirts, socks and ties. The shop appeared to have been made of several smaller shops thrown hastily into one. It was filled with doorways and corners and tiny flights of stairs in unlikely places, and there seemed to be no exit signs.

Soon Annabel became flustered and lost her sense of direction. She had planned to skirt the demonstration and reach the station from Parkin Street, but when finally she located a door and escaped into the open air, she found herself in a narrow road that was not Parkin Street, or any street she had ever seen before. There was hardly any traffic, and the sound of the demonstration seemed strangely distant, though surely it must have been just around the corner.

Most of the buildings were boarded up. Perhaps some sort of large-scale renovation was in progress. But right in front of Annabel, on the opposite side of the road, was a hairdressing establishment of a very superior kind. It appeared to be called simply, 'Mr Jerome'. On either side of its sumptuous entrance was an exquisitely groomed cumquat tree in a pot. Its window featured a strangely disturbing sculpture in chrome and three identical photographs of a very self-possessed young woman with gleaming golden hair—the sort of young woman who had no use for paperclips and had never eaten a fishfinger in her life.

Annabel had always known instinctively not to venture near such places, and would not have done so now, except that at that very moment the door opened. A top model, who had been featured on countless magazine covers, swept out, her mane of black hair freshly, and no doubt expensively, tousled.

Annabel gaped. She loved magazines, though she only ever read them second-hand. She had never seen a celebrity at such close quarters before. She realised that this was a brush with fame, of the sort she had heard callers on talkback radio mention, and she tried to remember the woman's name.

The woman looked thunderous as she towered in the doorway putting on her sunglasses, but as that was how she looked in all her photographs, this was no surprise.

What was a surprise was the tiny black kitten that shot out through the door, straight between the woman's elegant ankles. The woman did not notice it. Her head was much too far off the ground for her easily to see what was going on at her feet, and in any case she was looking at a long red car with tinted windows that was hurtling down the street towards her. She walked languidly to the edge of the pavement, the breeze of her long-legged passing spinning a dropped bus ticket into the gutter.

The black kitten looked alert, and pounced after it.

Annabel called out a warning, and stumbled onto the road, but the woman did not look around. Perhaps she was used to people calling out to her, or perhaps all that hair had a muffling effect. The car pulled up and idled gently as she got in. Just in front of its gigantic wheels, the black kitten patted the bus ticket, trying to make it come to life.

The car door slammed.

'No!' shrieked Annabel. She leaped the last few metres and slammed into the car's bonnet with some force, dropping her shopping and falling down on one knee. It's hard to save a life elegantly.

The car horn blasted and, startled, the kitten sprang into Annabel's arms. Clutching it, Annabel crawled to the pavement. The car, released, accelerated away, mashing the contents of Annabel's shopping bag to pulp.

At that moment a slim, bearded man, dressed dramatically in black and festooned with gold chains, came rushing from the salon uttering small cries of distress. Dazed as she was, Annabel could not help noticing that the purple streak in his flowing silver hair matched his nail polish exactly. She had no doubt that this was Mr Jerome himself.

'I saw it all!' the man cried, lifting Annabel from the pavement with one beautiful hand and gathering up the kitten with the other. 'I was simply *paralysed* with fear. Rooted to the spot, to coin a phrase! Me! Can you imagine? But you—you were so selfless! So brave! *Magnificent!*'

Annabel blushed and mumbled. The man's exotic appearance and manner made her very self-conscious.

'Oh, if anything had happened to Kitikins, *whatever*

would I have done?' the man went on. 'I've only had her a fortnight, and she's been coming on beautifully, too. He wagged his finger at the kitten, who was now curled, purring, on his shoulder. 'Naughty Kitikins!' he scolded. 'Don't you know you're precious?'

'Well,' said Annabel, beginning to edge away, glancing regretfully at her squashed shopping. 'I'd better . . .'

'But you can't go yet!' exclaimed the man, turning to her with glittering eyes. 'I must repay you! Choose your own reward. Anything in my power to give is yours!'

Annabel became convinced he wore mascara. And possibly eyeliner as well.

'It's really quite all right,' she said nervously but sincerely. 'I was pleased to help. I don't need any reward.'

'You *are* marvellous!' said the man, clasping his hands. 'But I *insist*. One good turn deserves another. That's an absolute *must*, in my book. Think, now. There must be *something* I could do for you.'

He looked so appealing that Annabel found herself trying to think of something. To accept money would be out of the question. But what else could this man do for her? Then she caught sight of the photographs in the salon window and a wonderful, daring idea came to her.

'Could . . . would you have time . . . would it be too much trouble . . . for you to make my hair gold?' she asked breathlessly.

'Easy as winking,' the man beamed. 'What a charming idea! A matching heart and hair set.' From his sleeve he drew a slim black stick that glowed at one end. 'Pay attention, Kitikins,' he shrilled, and waved the stick over Annabel's head. She felt a shivering thrill as though every hair was standing on end. Then the feeling was gone. But in the glass of the salon window she could see that her head was surrounded by a shining golden aureole.

She was very surprised. She thought it would have taken longer. Hairdressing had obviously taken great strides unknown to the ladies of Pompey's Family Hair Salon, where she usually had her hair cut.

'Gorgeous!' said the man. 'Now you be happy, dear, and then there won't be any nasty surprises in the regrowth.

A happy girl makes healthy hair, and who needs dull roots? To coin a phrase. Well, I must fly. Thanks again!'

And with that, he was gone.

Annabel blinked. She thought he must have gone back into the salon somehow, without her seeing. But when she looked inside she could see only a bored-looking girl sweeping scraps of purple and silver hair from the floor. And when she asked for Mr Jerome, the dark man with the ponytail who sauntered from the back room was a complete stranger to her.

'Oh, I'm sorry. I've made a mistake,' she said, confused. 'I was just talking to another gentleman from here—a man with silver and . . . um . . . purple hair. And a black kitten.'

'Gone and never called me mother,' the real Mr Jerome said airily. '*And* forgot to pay.'

'You mean he was just a *customer*?' gasped Annabel, astonished.

'A client,' corrected Mr Jerome. 'But never mind, he'll be back. He *adores* having his hair done.' He automatically cast a professional eye over Annabel's new hairdo, gave a small start, took a pair of glasses out of his pocket and peered at her. 'Would you care for a quick trim?' he asked abruptly. 'Or, how about a proper cut? Something lovely and short to beat the heat?'

'Oh, no, thank you,' stammered Annabel, evading his clutching hands and backing out the door as fast as she could. An oozing rain had begun and she put up the hood of her raincoat.

Mr Jerome ran after her. 'No charge,' she heard him bellowing as she hurried down the street, but she didn't turn around.

◇

Lawrence was very surprised when Annabel walked in the door, self-consciously pushing her rain hood back. But he rallied almost instantly, lay back against his pillows and said that he was glad she'd done something nice for herself, he hadn't had *too* bad a day, and what was for dinner? Then he went back to watching television.

As Annabel bent over the couch to kiss him he put up an absent-minded hand to ruffle her hair, as was his wont when he felt affectionate or when food was in the offing. Then he drew his hand back rather sharply and turned to look at her. Surprised, Annabel touched her hair herself and found that it was strangely cool, and even more wiry than usual.

'Who did this?' Lawrence spluttered. He turned off the TV. He was looking pale and shocked. He was, in fact, quite wild around the eyes. Annabel was very concerned. She thought he was probably worried about the cost, and hastened to reassure him by telling him the whole story. He didn't look bored once. In fact, he hung on her every word.

'This guy—he sounds like he was a fairy or something!' he exclaimed when she had finished.

Annabel said that she supposed he was a little bit effeminate—well, *very* effeminate, actually—but very nice.

Lawrence stared at her for a moment, then slumped down onto the couch and buried his face in his hands. The poor man is weak with hunger, Annabel thought, and hurried into the kitchen to start dinner. It would have to be macaroni cheese again.

But she had only had time to put the water on to boil when Lawrence came in. He looked carefully at her hair once more. Then he asked her to tell him once again what the man who wasn't Mr Jerome had said. Then he suggested they forget about the macaroni, and send out for pizza.

That night was the most romantic Annabel had ever experienced. By some happy chance Lawrence stumbled across a case of wine hidden in the cupboard under the stairs. Many of the bottles were empty, but there were still several that were full. Annabel was amazed. Lawrence said he thought a previous tenant must have left the wine, and they both exclaimed at their good luck. They sent out for pizza, salad *and* garlic bread. Lawrence said hang the expense.

Before they went to bed, he asked, quite nervously, if he could brush Annabel's hair, and shyly she agreed. It felt wonderful, and it was even more wonderful to see how tenderly he laid aside every hair that became caught in the brush. He said they would always remind him of the most wonderful night of his life.

The next day, Annabel woke to find that she had slept through the alarm. It was ten-thirty! She was just springing, horrified, out of bed when Lawrence came in, glowing, and told her that he had rung the factory and told them that she was ill, and would not be in to work.

He had already been out, it seemed. He said he had had an errand to do. On his way home he had picked up some croissants, some hazelnut chocolates (Annabel's favourite) and a bunch of pink carnations. He put the carnations in a vase and insisted on serving Annabel breakfast in bed. Then, when she had finished, he knelt beside her and, very sweetly, asked her to marry him.

'But, Lawrence,' breathed Annabel, her heart beating very fast 'I thought you said we couldn't afford to get married for years yet.'

Lawrence smoothed her tangled hair, whispered that one of his investments had finally paid off, and kissed her. Then he told her she was never to work again. He wanted her home, with him, for always. Now it was his time to work, and hers to rest. He had even made up a little poem for her, he said.

He repeated it softly.

> *Curly Locks, Curly Locks, wilt thou be mine?*
> *Thou shalt not wash dishes, nor yet feed the swine.*
> *But sit on a cushion, and read magazines,*
> *And feed upon croissants and hazelnut creams.*

Annabel liked Lawrence's version even better than her father's. She never had enjoyed sewing, and strawberries were only good at certain times of the year. 'I don't mind cooking for you, Lawrence,' she whispered. But Lawrence simply kissed her again, and picked a stray hair or two from her pillow with a dreamy smile.

After that, Annabel lived the life she had always longed for. Lawrence handled everything. His investments must have prospered, for gradually he and his wife became rich. They moved into a splendid house, with views of the sea, a heated swimming pool, a tennis court, a dishwasher and a self-cleaning oven. They had a TV set in every room and *Bogus* magazine on subscription. Surprisingly, after all he had said about religion's being the opiate of the masses, Lawrence became a Muslim and asked that Annabel cover her head whenever she went out. This didn't worry her at all, for he bought her all manner of beautiful scarves, turbans and snoods to wear on the rare occasions she wanted to go anywhere.

Every morning Lawrence served Annabel breakfast in

bed before hurrying away to see to their investments. Most afternoons they played tennis and swam a little, for exercise. Every night before bed he brushed her hair, and carried the brush away afterwards in clasped hands, as though every hair on her head was precious. It seemed to Annabel that his whole aim in life was to ensure that she remained content.

She was more than content. She was perfectly, even riotously, happy. And as a result, just as the strange man had told her, her hair continued to grow as thick and gold as ever, and never needed the roots done. Things had certainly moved on in the hairdressing industry.

She never went back to Mr Jerome's establishment. Or to Pompey's Family Hair Salon either. Lawrence insisted on cutting her hair himself. He always made a wonderful job of it. And he cleaned up beautifully afterwards.

Annabel wished that her parents could see how well things had turned out for her. She knew they'd be happy, but quite surprised.

Sometimes, curled up on the couch, talking to her

husband of old times, she'd remember her father putting her on his knee and saying, 'Bless your simple heart, Curly Locks. Ignorance is bliss.' Then she would sigh sentimentally, and Lawrence would anxiously adjust the cushion behind her golden head, beg her not to upset herself, and drop a tender kiss on her smooth brow before rushing off to make tea.

Annabel would smile, eat another hazelnut cream, open a magazine and wriggle with contentment.

Poor old Dad. Ignorance is bliss? Whatever *had* he meant?

Dr Knight and the Dragon

Once upon a time, a middle-aged associate professor called Knight, armoured only by his self-esteem, which was considerable, journeyed into a mountain wilderness to investigate rumours that a dragon was terrorising farmers, small shopkeepers and eco-tourists in the area.

Dr Knight took with him on his quest a good supply of tranquillising darts and his research assistant, Fenella. Fenella was young, naive, idealistic and very pretty in a reassuringly old-fashioned way. Ostensibly she was to assist by using the video camera, at which she was proficient, and by preparing the meals, but privately Knight had hopes that a few nights under the stars might encourage her to assist him in other, more personal, ways. Fenella was plainly fascinated by him, but unfortunately a Catholic upbringing in the suburbs had so far prevented her from taking her fascination to its logical conclusion.

Knight had made a study of mythical beasts and possessed a wide knowledge of their reputed habits. He was therefore looking forward to the task of tracking and, if possible, tagging the dragon, which he planned to name after himself. The video footage, with his laconic but erudite commentary, would, he was sure, be bought by one of the television networks, thus more than defraying the expenses of the trip and launching him into a new and profitable career as a media personality.

He made careful preparations for the expedition, purchasing a battered bushman's hat from his local St Vincent de Paul shop, having his beard trimmed, practising fire-lighting at night while his wife was at Red Cross meetings, and laying in a supply of mouthwash, condoms and Viagra. On the appointed day, he and Fenella drove to the walking track that was nearest to the dragon sightings and set off.

After half a day's trekking through wild and inhospitable countryside, Knight had three blisters but felt that he was definitely making progress. He had found no dragon, but Fenella had filmed him finding a chewed hiking boot, investigating several empty caves and staring thoughtfully into a pool. Along the way, he had managed to tell her casually that he and his wife were estranged.

That night, they pitched their tents in a clearing by a small stream. Knight lit a fire with commendable efficiency, and Fenella filmed him gazing thoughtfully into it.

They had eaten their frugal meal and drunk a good deal of wine, Fenella was sighing and giggling, and Knight had decided it might be time to delve into his sponge bag, when the bushes around the clearing rustled, and something moved out of the shadows and into the firelight.

It was a dragon.

It was small, but perfectly formed. Its green scales glittered. Its eyes were golden. It had spines on its back, a long tail and curved claws. When it breathed, a tiny glow of flame penetrated the darkness.

Fenella, very excited though afraid, bravely seized the camera and began filming. Knight, whose excitement had been up till then of quite another order, found it difficult to summon up much enthusiasm.

The dragon was far from being the huge, fearsome beast of legend. And when it began to speak, this, too, was a disappointment.

'Yummo! A maiden! Can I have a bit?' it asked Knight.

'Certainly not,' said Knight grumpily. 'It's mine!'

Fenella turned to him with glowing eyes. Her tender lips were slightly parted, and it seemed to Knight that the words 'My hero' were trembling upon them. All of a sudden he realised that fate had played into his hands.

He reached behind him for his supply of tranquillising darts. Puny the dragon might be, but still it was a dragon. If he could slay it, metaphorically, his future, sexual in the short term, professional in the long term, was assured.

The dragon began to whine. 'Oh, go on!' it said. 'Give us some! Don't be mean!'

'There is no way in the world that you are going to eat my research assistant,' said Knight firmly, fitting a dart into his gun.

'Will!' said the dragon, stamping its foot.

'Won't!' said Knight, and, smiling grimly, he fired.

The dart flew through the air, hit the dragon's scaly back and bounced off, falling bent and harmless to the ground.

The dragon giggled.

Knight became slightly nervous. He fired another dart with the same effect. That is, no effect at all. The dragon hissed and moved threateningly towards Fenella. With a shriek, Fenella dropped the video camera and ran behind Knight, clutching at his shirt in terror.

The dragon moved nearer. Its golden eyes were burning with anger. Knight put his hand behind him and tried to prise Fenella's rigid fingers loose.

'Ah . . . Fenella,' he murmured. 'It might be better if

you stood a little further away, sweetie—to give me more freedom of movement.'

But Fenella, screaming wildly now, would not let go. The dragon lunged forward.

'You're so mean! I'll get you!' it screeched. Its jaws snapped. Its hot breath seared Knight's face, and the smell of singed hair mingled with the fragrant smoke of the campfire, his own aftershave and sweat, and the warm scent of Fenella's trembling body.

Dr Knight was just about to tear the girl off his back, breaking her fingers if necessary, and throw her to the beast, when he noticed something.

The dragon's teeth were not very big. In fact, they were extremely small. Its talons bent where they touched the ground. And after that one burst of heat, its fire seemed to have become exhausted. A few little wisps of smoke were dribbling from its mouth, but that was all.

In other words, this dragon was plainly a degenerate example of its species. It would be a pushover.

He made an instant, and inspired, decision.

'Fenella,' he said in a firm, low voice. 'Listen to me carefully. Slip your hand into my left-hand trouser pocket. Feel around until you find my car keys.'

Breathing hard, Fenella did as he asked. Her feverish gropings were extremely pleasant, and Knight was breathing pretty hard himself by the time she found his key ring.

'When I say "Go", I want you to run,' he told her. 'I will cover you. Run as fast as you can, sweet girl, to the car, and go for help. And don't look back.'

'No, Gavin, I won't leave you!' cried Fenella.

Knight drew himself up. 'You must,' he said, in a low, throbbing voice. 'Now, go!'

He felt the girl's soft lips press against his sunburned neck for a single moment. And then, with a choking sob, she was gone.

Knight and the dragon listened to her fading footfalls. The dragon's lips quivered and it stamped its foot.

'Look what you've done!' it bawled. 'Now she's got away. And I haven't had a maiden for ages and ages.'

'Stop that! You're hysterical!' snapped Knight, in the

voice he reserved for his most irritating students and his wife. Now he was in for a boring few hours waiting for Fenella to return. But at the end of that time—as she showed her gratitude for his heroism in some cosy little mountain guesthouse—it would be worth it.

The dragon was still mumbling and whingeing in a most annoying way.

Knight picked up a stout stick, which was fortuitously lying by his feet, and smacked the whining green muzzle.

'Clear off!' he snapped.

Tears sprang into the dragon's eyes, and it backed away. Then it began to shriek and roar. 'He hit me!' it cried. 'The big, bad bully took my maiden, and then he hit me! Whaa!'

At that moment, Dr Knight felt the ground begin to shake. He saw something very amazing rise above the trees. For the first time in his life he had a small twinge of self-doubt—the tiniest inkling that perhaps he had miscalculated.

It was unpleasant, but he didn't have to bear it for long.

The last thing he heard in this world was the little dragon's final screech:

'Get him! Get him, Mamma!'

The Fat Wife

Once upon a time there was a woman called Rosemary who had a pretty face, a sweet and generous nature, and a weight problem.

Rosemary had fought her problem in many ways. She had tried numerous diets, including the Israeli army diet, and stuck to none of them. She had followed advice in popular magazines, invested large sums in patent slimming foods, pills and devices, and joined several weight-loss programs, to no avail. She once considered liposuction, but shortly afterwards saw, in *Slimmers World*, some step-by-step photographs of the procedure, and dropped the idea.

Rosemary had been on the plump side since girlhood but when, at the age of nineteen, she had met and married her husband, a lean and hungry law student called Paul, she had been a relatively respectable size 12. In fifteen years of marriage she had ballooned, jerkily but relentlessly, to her present size 18, and took care never to be photographed from the side. Her modest wardrobe consisted almost entirely of black outfits featuring below-the-hip jackets and strong neckline interest. The only exception was a leopard-skin patterned crossover number she had bought one day when she was premenstrual, and in which she resembled a strong man in a circus.

A receptionist by trade, Rosemary had supported her husband through his final years of study and early struggles at the bar. Now he was a successful corporate lawyer, and earned far more money than she did. She wasn't quite sure how much more, because they had separate bank accounts, but of course he always paid his share of the mortgage and housekeeping.

Paul had never wanted a family, and, though very

disappointed, for she was a loving and maternal woman with good child-bearing hips, Rosemary had agreed that it was best for them to remain childless. Paul left the house at seven-thirty every morning and often wasn't home until nine-thirty or ten at night—sometimes much later because of business dinners, which seemed to make him terribly tired—and a child deserved a full-time father.

Paul was a proud man, and ashamed of his chubby wife, who ruined his modern, youthful image. He knew that the time was coming when he would have to trade her in. Already he was planning ahead, by transferring all his assets to the various loss-making companies he had set up over the years.

Rosemary knew how her husband felt, and shed many bitter tears over it. Each morning, after he had left for work, a well-shaved, youthful, aggressive vision in silk tie and Armani suit, hair well-moussed, she felt that her heart was breaking as she stacked his muesli plate and fruit juice glass into the dishwasher, picked up his wet towel from the bathroom floor, and hung his jogging gear out to air.

Then, while the scent of his cologne still wafted in the breakfast nook, she comforted herself with coffee, many chocolate chip cookies and several rounds of peanut butter toast before struggling into one of the black outfits that still met around her waist, and leaving for her own job at Smart, Grimm and Greesy, chartered accountants.

Messrs Smart, Grimm and Schitie (Greesy was long dead) would have preferred that Rosemary was not quite so tubby, but privately agreed that, despite her appearance, she was a treasure. Her motherly demeanour comforted nervous clients, her sweet smile soothed aggressive clients, and her sense of humour kept the staff sweet. She had a first-aid certificate, which was often useful, and could deal with the temperamental office lift, a talent which on several occasions had saved the firm severe embarrassment and possibly legal action. Also, she did not demand a high salary, because she thought it was very kind of SG & G to keep her on.

One morning, Paul made his move, having packed his bags and put them into the car the night before while

Rosemary was asleep. After breakfast he read a prepared statement, warning her that the antiques and original artworks in the house were the property of one of his companies and could not be sold without the authority of the directors. Then he left.

Rosemary wept as she put her soon-to-be-ex husband's muesli plate and fruit juice glass in the dishwasher, picked up his wet towel from the bathroom floor, and hung out his jogging clothes to air. Then she ate a pack of chocolate chip cookies, some marshmallows and a cold meat pie she found at the back of the fridge, struggled into the one black day outfit that still met around her waist, and went to work.

It was a day like any other, except that she felt numb and her heart was like a cold lump of lead in her breast. The numbness lifted briefly on only one occasion, when she freed a new client, a small dark man called Mr Shahim, from the lift. Mr Shahim was a sole trader in the entertainment business, and was most grateful for his release—it seemed that he was claustrophobic due to some previous traumatic experience in his life. Rosemary was sympathetic, and gave him tea and two of her own sugar biscuits, to settle his nerves, before taking him to Mr Schitie's office. Then she went back to work, the numb feeling returned, and slowly the time passed.

When she arrived home that evening there was a 'For Sale' sign on the front lawn of the house.

Paul moved into a city apartment that he had bought in one of his company names, pulled strings and fiddled dates to have the divorce heard as quickly as possible, and found a size 8 girlfriend with long blonde hair and an MBA.

Rosemary stayed on in the house, keeping it clean and fresh-smelling for prospective buyers, and went to SG & G every day. At the same time, she went on a diet of her own devising. This involved eating radishes, grated carrot, tuna and cottage cheese, standing up, three times a day, and only broken cookies, stale cake, the unbruised parts of bruised bananas and cold toast in between. She did not lose weight, but went up a shoe size. She was very unhappy, but knew she could only blame herself.

When the house was sold, she moved into a compact bachelor flat convenient to public transport, meaning that it was one room with cooking facilities and bathroom, and on a main road. It was only a few doors away from SG & G, so, with her travelling time reduced, she had more leisure time. This she didn't find an enormous advantage.

Fortunately, her working hours were busy and full. She dealt with the phone, and with the clients, including Mr Shahim, who was now a regular visitor and sat patiently on the black vinyl couch in the reception area each month, his hands quietly folded and his liquid brown eyes staring into space. She collected for staff birthday cakes and flowers, gave paracetamol to girls with period pain and first aid to juniors who had jammed their fingers in filing cabinets. She sympathised with people who had suffered reverses in love or whose dogs had been run over.

And of course she joined the office buzz when Mr

Schitie secured a ticket to the charity event of the year, the Ear-wax Buildup Research Foundation's Friday the 13th Gala Magic Ball. Mr Schitie's own daughter had been a sufferer of ear-wax buildup, and SG & G was a minor sponsor of the charity, but he was still lucky to have reached the B list. Invitations were like gold. Mr Schitie, who was rather a social climber, was cock-a-hoop, and subsequently managed to work at least one reference to the approaching date into every conversation.

Rosemary also had the date circled on her desk calendar, because, by chance, it was the same day that her divorce was to become final. This was rather an irony, she thought, though she tried not to dwell on it.

When the day came, she spent her lunchtime having her wedding ring removed. She went back to the office trying to forget the jeweller's thin-lipped distaste, and to hide her finger, which now looked like a reddened and badly dented sausage.

She quickly forgot her personal troubles, however, for soon after his own return from lunch, Mr Schitie fell over in the men's room and broke his ankle. Someone said he was drunk, but Rosemary knew that this couldn't be true. Mr Schitie had always spoken very strongly against drinking in working hours, and had actually sacked Sylvia from accounts for getting tiddly on her twenty-first birthday. Besides, he had been having lunch with Mr Shahim, who did not drink alcohol.

Rosemary called the ambulance and, with her usual caring efficiency, did what she could to relieve Mr Schitie's pain while they waited for it to arrive.

As he was carried away by the paramedics, Mr Schitie pressed his Ear-wax Magic Ball ticket into Rosemary's hand.

'You been good to me, Rosie,' he slurred. 'You take it. Represhent the firm.'

'Oh, thank you, Mr Schitie,' gasped Rosemary, her plump face flushing with pleasure.

'You're a good woman,' he moaned, gripping her hand. 'Fat, but good. Oh, God, my ankle! That last Marguerita . . .'

Which seemed strange to Rosemary, because his wife's name was Leonie.

At home that evening Rosemary showered, did her hair, made up her face, dressed carefully in her best blacks and ate two radishes and half a loaf of cold toast. Then she put on fresh lipstick and her mother's pearls and made her way to the ballroom of the Palace-Hilton, where the Ear-wax Gala was in full swing.

It was a glittering affair in every way. In concert with the magic theme, silver stars and baubles hung from the ballroom ceiling below the famous glass dome, the dance band members were wearing silver jackets, and jugglers, contortionists, magicians and mime artists were performing on small silver platforms all around the walls. A larger platform, set in the middle of the dance floor and hung with gold, was empty, waiting for the main attraction.

The crowd was also glittering. There were many celebrities present—Vicki from Pick-a-Barrel, Roy Smudge, the controversial property developer who had narrowly escaped death by letter bomb, the youth with the ponytail from the

Chunky Bix ad and the Minister for Ear, Nose and Throat, to name a few. There were also several swarthy, bearded men in long, flowing robes, honoured guests from a small Arab emirate, who had been fobbed off on the Minister for the evening.

Rosemary had just managed to secure a glass of champagne from the tray of a passing waiter when her stomach seemed to turn over. Paul was standing on the other side of the room. Their eyes met, but his immediately slid away as if he did not recognise her. He was with his blonde size 8 and two other couples who looked exactly like them. Of course, he did not want to be embarrassed by acknowledging her. Someone might have asked who she was.

Rosemary felt her face burning. She gulped at her champagne and it went straight to her head. A waiter, more sympathetic than the last one had been, took her empty glass and replaced it with a full one. She drank that, too, then looked around for the exit.

But at that moment the lights dimmed, a spotlight went on over the central podium, and there was a drum roll. Plainly, the main entertainment was about to begin. Rosemary knew that it would be impossibly rude to leave now. She would have to wait.

'Ladies and gentlemen,' a voice boomed over the loudspeaker. 'Please welcome the astounding, the amazing, the unforgettable—Shahim the Great!'

Rosemary's jaw dropped as Mr Shahim—the very Mr Shahim who had sat so often on the black vinyl couch in the reception area of SG & G—climbed into the spotlight to scattered applause. He was wearing a rather shabby dark blue robe and turban instead of his usual rather shiny dark blue suit, but otherwise he looked exactly the same. Small, thin and nervous.

'Where'd they dig him up?' a woman behind Rosemary muttered to her neighbour.

Mr Shahim cleared his throat and spoke into the microphone, which whistled piercingly. He looked worried, the crowd murmured, and Rosemary blushed for him. He adjusted the microphone and spoke again in his low, hesitating voice.

'It has been some time since I performed in the public arena, and I beg your indulgence. I will need an assistant. Could I have a volunteer from among the good ladies here tonight?'

No one moved. Mr Shahim stood waiting patiently, his hands folded and his dark, liquid eyes searching the room. The silence lengthened.

Rosemary felt quite desperately sorry for him. If only she had known ahead of time, she could have warned him that no woman in this cool crowd would ever expose herself by volunteering for anything, let alone for something that invited certain ridicule.

Mr Shahim spread his small brown hands. 'Please,' he said simply, and it seemed to Rosemary that his eyes met hers with mute appeal. Then the eyes seemed to flash, and her heart lurched.

She stepped forward. 'I will,' she said clearly.

She heard the muffled titters as she clumped to the platform, aware of a hundred pairs of eyes on her vast black behind, a hundred pairs of eyes on her bolster-like front, and a hundred pairs of eyes on each of her regrettably bulging profiles. Mr Shahim smiled at her gravely as he helped her up the steps and led her to the centre of the podium.

'Good,' he said. 'Now we can begin. But first . . .'

He raised his hand over Rosemary's head. A shower of blinding silver sparks sprayed from his fingers. The people gasped and covered their eyes. When they looked again, Rosemary had been transformed. A shining peacock-blue robe floated around her. Filmy silver veils wafted gently with her every movement. Tiny, jewelled bells tinkled on her wrists, around her ankles, in her ears and through her hair. Her eyes were huge with glitter and shadow. Her lips were rich and red.

She was large. She was luscious. She was beautiful.

One of the robed men standing with the Minister hissed something under his breath, and licked his lips. The Minister looked shocked.

Thunderous applause broke out, but Shahim the Great barely acknowledged it, because by now he was filling the air above the platform with doves and rainbows, twining the columns of the ballroom with vines, and making flowers spring from the gold-draped boards beneath Rosemary's feet. He took the pipe she handed him and blew two huge bubbles of pink light, from which stepped two winged white horses with flowing golden manes, each with a huge basket of red roses on either side of its broad back.

Then he pressed the palms of his hands together, and bowed. And Rosemary, flushed and smiling, her arms full of roses, bowed too. As did the horses.

The cheers and clapping went on and on, until finally the Emir's representative stepped forward and held up his hands for silence.

'Shahim's powers we know,' he said, in strongly accented but perfect English. 'He is an old friend, though I had not expected to see him here. But this woman . . . is magnificent. A woman such as this would be worth her weight in rubies to any man. And in her case, the weight is considerable.'

Shahim the Great nodded. 'As you say,' he said gravely.

'Then let it be done!' said the Emir's representative.

Shahim lifted his hand. Again there was a shower of sparks, but red this time. And when the sparks cleared, the baskets on the horses' backs were groaning with huge, glittering rubies.

The crowd moaned in wonder and avarice.

'Who has the good fortune to have this lady for a wife?' demanded the Emir's representative. 'Now he will be rich in more ways than one.'

Paul lurched forward, treading on his size 8's foot as he did so, and breaking two of her toes.

'She's mine!' he shouted. 'My wife! Mine!'

But, dreamily, Rosemary shook her head. 'I am not married,' she said.

And with that, Shahim took her hand and together they floated onto the backs of the horses, landing as lightly as rose petals on the shoulders of a bride. Then the horses spread their shining wings and flew up, up into the air, past the silver stars and the baubles, past the concealed light fittings and up to the top of the great glass dome, through which they passed as though it were mist.

Looking up, the crowd saw them for a moment outlined against the moon, their robes fluttering in the breeze of their horses' wings.

And then they were gone.

Red roses scattered behind them as they flew into the warm, starry night. Rosemary preferred flowers to rubies, and Shahim the Great would always give her what her heart desired. For him, precious gems were an everyday affair, but the love of a good and ample woman was something that even a genie could not provide for himself. Like her beauty, it had had to be discovered. Like his freedom, it had had to be earned. And, as Shahim treasured freedom and beauty, so he would treasure love, for as long as he and his precious Rose lived.

Which would be for some considerable time, and would involve exotic locations, untold wealth and much laughter. Also, a lot of passionate sex and many children.

You know how genies are.

Justin and the Troll

Once there was a well-groomed and well-meaning young man called Justin who fancied himself tired of city life. One fine winter weekend, he and his girlfriend, Lucy, travelled to Wilson Reach, a small and picturesque town on the south coast that Justin had read about in the travel section of the Saturday newspaper.

Lucy, who was not at all tired of city life, had agreed to go on the trip only because she loved Justin. Normally, wild horses would not have dragged her away from reliable hot water and streetlights that stayed on all night. Suffering overseas was stimulating and a source of good anecdotes. Suffering in one's own country was futile.

It was a long, long drive, begun in the energy, jokes and laughter of early love, continued in the sporadic conversation and stiffness of sorely tried affection, and finished in the silence of grim endurance. Lucy had made Justin stop three times—first, so that she could buy mineral water; second, so she could go to a King's Famous Fritzburger ladies' room; and third, so that he could put his Afghan peasant vest, ideal for winter country wear, in the boot, because the reek of poorly tanned goat hide was making her carsick. But at last they arrived at Wilson Reach.

It was a sweet and dusty town with a single main street, pepper trees, a war memorial and painted awnings over the shops. Justin found it slightly disappointing only because it looked exactly like all the towns they'd passed through in the last two hours. Lucy was just glad to have arrived.

They found the Wilson Reach Hotel, where they were booked for the night, with no difficulty, since it was the only hotel in the town. There was also a Flag Inn, on the outskirts, but Justin had eschewed that, preferring the old-style country pub that the newspaper article had spoken of in such glowing terms.

Possibly the travel writer had stayed at the Wilson Reach Hotel under different management, or perhaps, as Lucy bitterly remarked, hauling her bag up the narrow, evil-smelling stairs to their hot little room with its cabbage rose wallpaper, he had never stayed there at all, but simply driven past it.

Whatever, the promised warm country welcome was there in plenty, if the warm country comfort was a little lacking. Once they were settled in room 13, the landlady showed them to the beer garden—which had white wrought-iron furniture, only slightly rusty, and a wonderful view of the river—and brought them ham sandwiches and glasses of soda water with lemon slices speared on the rims. If the ham tasted like the fridge, the bread was curled at the corners, and the lemon had plainly been cut for about a fortnight, these were pointless quibbles as far as Justin was concerned. He had recently decided that city people made too much fuss about food.

After lunch, they went for a walk through the town to soak up the atmosphere. It didn't take very long. In about ten minutes they found themselves at the last shopfront. A real estate agent's office.

Justin was fascinated by all the properties displayed in the window. They were so cheap! He could hardly believe how cheap they were. He could have bought any one of them with the deposit he had so far saved against the day when he would buy a warehouse conversion apartment in the city.

There was one in particular . . . The faded photograph showed a cute white cottage, its verandah overgrown with honeysuckle in full bloom. The label read:

> *ACREAGE! FISH YOUR OWN*
> *TROUT STREAM!*
> *Your dreams can come true in 'Honeysuckle Cottage'.*
>
> *Cute 2-bed w/board cottage packed with all the*

*charm of yesteryear. Rambling gardens, native
bushland, trout stream, peace and tranquillity.
   Why wait?*

Lucy said that meant the place was a wreck, with an outside toilet, a run-down garden and uncleared land beyond. She pointed out that the photograph was so faded, the place had probably been empty for years, and for good reason. She also suggested, quite forcibly, that they should go back to the hotel.

But Justin's imagination was seized. He felt that the little white cottage was somehow calling him. He decided that he'd go into the real estate office and ask about it.

Lucy left him to it, darkly warning him not to lose his head.

There was only one person in the real estate office: a sharp-eyed woman with curly, bright red hair that contrasted strangely with her brown, weather-beaten face. She told Justin that her name was Val.

When she heard that he was interested in viewing Honeysuckle Cottage, her eyes narrowed slightly and she said that, my word, he could pick a bargain. She said that she was on her own at present, so couldn't take him to view, but that Honeysuckle Cottage was empty, the key was under the front doormat, and Justin could let himself in. The owner had some stuff locked up in the cellar, she said, so she'd trouble Justin not to go in there, but otherwise he could poke around all he liked. They were very casual in the country. She smiled, showing many large, tobacco-stained teeth.

Justin asked the address, and, without losing her smile, Val said that there wasn't an address, as such, which he found charming. She showed him a map of the area, then drew him a sketch map on the back of a piece of office stationery. Her suggested route would take him back up the highway and across the river by the Greater Pooner punt that left on the half-hour.

'Surely there'd be another crossing that's nearer, if I went on past here, to the south?' Justin asked. He prided himself on his map-reading abilities. 'I mean, the river bends and narrows just a little way beyond town. There seem to be all sorts of little roads and so on around there. There must be a ford, or a bridge or something.'

Val flapped her hand dismissively and said that oh, there were little crossings the locals used—that Justin himself would use, no doubt, if he bought a property here. But it all depended on the weather, and the crossings were hard to find anyway, and he shouldn't bother about that now.

He thanked her, took her map, and left. But when, a few minutes later, she saw him drive his little red Toyota past the shopfront, heading south, she sighed.

'You should've told him it was no go, whatever he bloody said,' grunted her partner, Ed, who had come back in the interim. 'It's like a red rag to a bull, telling a city bloke about local roads he won't be able to work out. That's the second time you've done that, Val, and both times you've come undone.'

The woman shrugged. 'Maybe he'll get lost,' she said hopefully.

Ed shook his head. 'We won't see him again,' he growled. 'One way or the other.'

Ten minutes later, Justin was crawling through a maze of narrow tracks to the south of town, telling himself that there was no way an entire river could disappear, as this one seemed to have done.

Finally he passed a house where a man in a checked shirt was leaning over the front fence, chewing his gums and staring into space.

Justin swallowed his pride, pulled up, showed the man the map, and asked the way to Honeysuckle Cottage, across the river.

'You'd be meaning the old Sluggan place, mate,' the man said authoritatively.

Justin wasn't sure.

'It would be,' the man said. 'Honeysuckle's bloody near pulled it down, the Sluggan place. When they carried old Mick Sluggan out, they could hardly get him through the door. They say. 'Course, he was stiff as a board.'

'Is it for sale?' Justin asked desperately. 'The Sluggan place?'

The man in the checked shirt nodded. 'Oh, it's for *sale*,' he said. 'Interested, are ya?'

Justin, carefully, said he might be. But he couldn't seem to find a way across the river.

The man told him he wanted to go back to Wilson Reach, drive north along the highway and take the Greater Pooner punt, which went on the half-hour.

'But surely there's a quicker way from here?' said Justin, whose experience with telephone banking had taught him to be persistent and patient. 'Isn't there a bridge?'

'Oh, there's a *bridge*,' said the man. He jerked his head along the road. 'Just along past here. But—'

With a word of thanks, Justin started the car. As he

drove away, he heard the man call after him: 'But you wouldn't want to go that way, mate. There's a toll.'

Justin lifted his finger laconically, in the country manner, and drove on, smiling to himself. Independent old bastard, he thought indulgently. Rather spend twice the money on petrol going the long way than pay a toll. Well, that's what they're like in the bush. That's what's so great about them.

The man looked after him, chewing his gums. After a while he walked back to the house. His wife met him on the verandah.

'What'd he want?' she asked, jerking her head towards the road.

'Wanted to know where the bridge was,' said the man, levering off his boots with a groan.

'Didn't you tell him about the troll?' his wife demanded.

The man shrugged. 'He didn't seem to worry about it,' he said. 'You know what these blow-ins are like. Can't tell them anything.'

And he went inside.

Meanwhile, Justin was bumping along the road with a rising sense of elation. He felt he was defeating all odds to reach his goal. When he bought Honeysuckle Cottage, he told himself, he'd buy a four-wheel-drive. He laughed, took a sip of mineral water, and reminded himself not to lose his head.

After a while he reached the bridge. It looked rather old and rickety and, to his surprise, there was no sign of a tollgate. Nevertheless, he eased the car's wheels onto the creaking boards. He was about halfway across when a powerful, half-naked figure leaped in ungainly fashion onto the bonnet, landing with a crash.

The car's airbags instantly inflated, hitting Justin violently in the face and flattening him against the back of his seat. Justin yelled, and jammed his foot on the brake.

The windscreen shattered under the impact of a huge fist, and there was a ripping sound as the swollen fabric in front of him was torn apart. Then his attacker was glaring at him through the windscreen. He was very ugly and very hairy, with bulging muscles, a humped back and large, yellow, pointed teeth, which were bared in a hideous scowl.

Justin began to have some second thoughts about his putative neighbours. Inbreeding was the phrase that leaped to mind. The eyes were very close together. And those teeth . . .

The invader on the bonnet leaned forward menacingly and grabbed Justin by the throat.

Justin realised that the situation was serious.

'I bite your head off now!' growled the troll, pushing pieces of the shattered windshield away with his free hand.

'Hey, no! Hey, don't do that,' gurgled Justin, fumbling for his wallet. 'Look, you can have whatever you want. Okay? Cash, credit cards—the CD? Whatever you want.'

The troll paused. 'Got any sheep?' he demanded, pushing forward to scan the inside of the car.

Justin shook his head, trying not to wince. The troll's breath was terrible.

'Geese?' asked the troll, smacking his lips. 'Little pig? New calf—Jersey, for choice?'

'No,' said Justin.

'Have to be your head, then,' said the troll. He raised his fist, beat out the last of the windscreen and started to haul Justin out through the gap.

Justin caught at the wheel of the car with one hand and held it fast. The troll hauled, grunting. Justin clung, strangling. He thought he was probably losing consciousness. A vision of Lucy lying languidly on the bed in the Wilson Reach Hotel rose before his panic-stricken eyes. And with this vision came a last, despairing thought.

'Goat!' he croaked. 'How . . . you feel about—goat?'

The troll stopped heaving. 'Goat?' he grumbled. 'Don't talk to me 'bout goat. No bloody goats round here for years.'

'I . . . got . . . goat,' rasped Justin. He managed to reach the boot lock with one of his toes. The boot clicked open.

The troll sniffed. First suspiciously, then eagerly.

'See? Good goat,' choked Justin. 'Want it? You want it?'

The troll, unable to contain himself, jumped off the bonnet and lumbered to the back of the car. He tore the Afghan peasant vest out of the boot and wrestled it to the side of the road, joyously sinking his teeth into the noisome, embroidered skin, the matted, odoriferous hair.

Justin slammed the car into reverse and got out of there.

The man in the checked shirt saw him haring past, boot flapping. He lifted a hand in casual greeting, but Justin didn't stop.

'Unfriendly lot, these blow-ins,' the man said to his wife as he walked back inside.

◇

Not long afterwards, Val saw Justin's car clanking slowly past the real estate agent's office, heading for the Wilson Reach Hotel.

'He's back,' she called to Ed, who was cutting his toenails in the back room.

'Troll didn't get him, then?' said Ed.

'No,' said Val, peering through the door after the stuttering car. 'But he's not coming in.' She sighed, and lit another cigarette.

'He'd never have bought Sluggan's, anyway. Once he saw what was in the cellar,' her partner observed.

'No.' Val sighed again. 'We'll never sell that place, you know, Ed,' she said.

'Nah,' Ed agreed. 'Still, ya can't win 'em all.'

◇

Jason trudged up the stairs of the Wilson Reach Hotel and knocked at the door of room 13.

Lucy opened it, wearing only a very small pink camisole, and he fell into her arms.

'Justin, you've been ages!' she cried, hugging him, because she really did love him very much, and had been worried. Then, as he clung to her, her eyes narrowed. 'You didn't lose your head, did you?' she asked.

'No,' mumbled Justin into her shoulder. And then, because he was an honest young man, he added: 'But it was a near thing.'

Angela's Mandrake

Once there was a sweet and pretty merchant banker called Angela who was very unlucky in love. A succession of disastrous relationships with faithless men had sapped her faith in herself and in life to such an extent that on her thirty-ninth birthday she began to hear voices urging her to take a machine gun and mow down anyone with an Adam's apple who used the word 'commitment'.

Realising that her state of mind was somewhat unhealthy, she took leave from work and had herself admitted to a psychiatric institution.

Her therapist was a brisk but sympathetic woman of

forty-five who secretly felt that Angela's voices' opinions had a lot to commend them. All the same, mass murder was not socially acceptable by any standards, and she had her duty to do.

After six weeks under her care, Angela no longer heard the voices and was pronounced cured. Her therapist recommended that, on her return to the outside world, she take up an absorbing and relaxing hobby such as rock climbing, golf or gardening.

Since rocks tended to be hard and pointed, and golf featured balls, Angela decided that gardening was the most appealing of the options offered. Besides, she had already decided to sell her inner-city apartment, which had been totally redecorated, at her expense, by Russell, her last boyfriend. Russell had been an unemployed theatrical set designer: theatrical in both senses. The hard-edged grey, white and black leather theme that he had insisted expressed her personality had always depressed her, and she knew she could never again go into the ensuite where, on Christmas Eve, she had discovered him cavorting with her Uncle Gervase.

She bought a small house in a quiet suburb and, labouring after work and on weekends, began transforming its buffalo grass, cactus and concrete surrounds into a garden. Since she was hardworking and efficient in everything she did, and had far more talent than she gave herself credit for, the garden soon became a thing of beauty. This gave Angela great satisfaction, and made her many friends in the street. She was soon contributing potted specimens to the quarterly Red Cross plant stall and swapping stories and cuttings at the garden club, which met on the third Tuesday of every month.

Seven years passed, and Angela's garden was a symphony of pastels and perfume. It had pools where waterlilies bloomed, and shady bowers where violets clustered. Fragrant herbs nestled among its groves of slender trees. Birds sang and insects hummed on the margins of its winding paths and in the delicate haze of its secret places. It was a byword in the district, had been photographed for garden and lifestyle magazines several times, and had featured on television as well. It made an excellent makeover story, for Angela had efficiently taken and kept all the 'before' photographs. The transformation filled people with wonder.

'This garden is magic!' visitors would say. And Angela, walking in the cool of the evening amid the peace and beauty of the small paradise she had created, had no difficulty in believing it.

She still had lingering regrets about her single status, however, and one winter was persuaded by a well-meaning friend to take a ten-day South Sea Islands cruise. The friend had met her own husband this way and, though they were now divorced, still recommended it highly as a method of finding a mate.

Angela's ship was filled with rugby teams having bonding sessions, businessmen having bonding sessions, and retired couples. There were also six single women and five single men. The singles walked around eyeing one another for a couple of days, then paired off quite suddenly, as if by mutual consent, leaving a gaunt blonde divorcee called Beth stranded and alone as if she was the loser in a game of musical chairs.

Angela's pair was a divorced dentist called Greg. He was on the heavy side, and ten years older than her, but he was ruggedly handsome in some lights and had wavy, iron-grey hair and very clean nails. He had come on the cruise to get away from his patients for a while. Some of them, he said, were extremely neurotic. His receptionist, furthermore, had recently walked out without notice, leaving a dead goldfish on the waiting room carpet. It was very hard to get reliable help.

When Greg asked her to his cabin for a drink late on the fourth night, Angela felt she was ready to accept. She was not, however, ready to accept his post-drink request that she put on the rubber crotchless trousers, mask and surgical gloves he apparently found necessary for successful intimacy, and they parted awkwardly almost immediately afterwards.

Her subsequent days on the ship were spent enjoying

the sea air, reading, making interesting tours of hibiscus nurseries at various ports of call, and trying not to think about what Greg and Beth were doing in his cabin each night.

◇

Finally the cruise was over and Angela was able to return home. She arrived at dusk. Her garden whispered around the house, full of magic and secrets. There was something different about the atmosphere. She could not put her finger on it, but she felt it acutely. She put her bags in the house and went out to see what was doing.

She saw nothing unusual until she reached the side of the house where she had made a small pool surrounded by pink violets. She had always planned to have a white magnolia beside the pool, so that the flowers would be reflected in the water, but somehow she had never got around to it, and had let the violets have their way.

But now, leering at her from right in the middle of the violet-clad space, was a rank and aggressive weed!

Her nose wrinkling with distaste, Angela stepped forward to pull out the intruder by the roots. But just as she grasped it, a voice at her feet croaked:

'I wouldn't do that if I were you.'

Angela jumped back with a scream. Then she looked down and saw a small brown frog looking at her from the edge of the pool.

'That's a mandrake,' said the frog. 'If you pull it out it will scream. And if you hear a mandrake scream, you die. Take my word for it. If not for your own sake, for your neighbours'. There's a baby in the house next door, too.'

Angela stared, opening and closing her mouth. Her first thought was that never, never could she tell anyone about this, or she'd end up back in the looney bin. Her second thought was that she was overtired. She turned and, pretending she hadn't heard the frog's farewell, went back into the house. There she drank two glasses of rum and milk, unpacked her bags, did two loads of washing, and went to bed. At 3 am she got up and looked up 'mandrake' in *The Compleat Herbal*. The information it gave was not reassuring. The frog, it seemed, was right.

The following day was Saturday. At the crack of dawn, Angela put on her gardening gloves, took her sharpest secateurs, and went around to the pond at the side of the house.

The mandrake was bigger than ever. The frog was much the same size as it had been the day before.

'I wouldn't use those,' said the frog, eyeing Angela's secateurs nervously. 'It'll scream its lungs out if you cut it. Mandrakes can't stand pain. Especially of that kind.'

'I don't believe this,' snapped Angela. 'It's absurd superstition. And I don't believe you're talking to me, either. Frogs can't talk.'

'Aha!' said the frog slyly. 'But I'm not just an ordinary

frog. You've transformed this garden. It's magic. Haven't you been told that, over and over again?'

Angela returned to the house knowing that he spoke the truth. She went back to bed, but it was impossible to rest. She kept thinking of the mandrake's big fat taproot, plunging deeper into her soft, friable soil every moment she lay there helpless.

She stayed inside all day, thinking. In the late afternoon she grabbed her handbag and rushed out. At nightfall she returned with a large-sized pump pack of weedkiller. She had never used a herbicide before, heavy mulching being her preferred method of weed control, but this was an emergency.

'What's that?' said the frog when she arrived at the pool with her weapon

'Poison,' said Angela, through gritted teeth. 'I am going to poison this mandrake. It will die slowly, therefore it will not scream. The most I expect is a low groan. This may go on for some time, but at least it won't strike the baby next door dead. Or me, for that matter.'

She turned to the mandrake, her index finger poised on the trigger of the weedkiller pump-pack.

The mandrake stood, lonely and proud, its leaves stiff and upright. Behind it, the full moon rose. The whole garden seemed to hold its breath.

Angela lowered her arm.

'What's wrong?' demanded the frog. 'Don't you want to get rid of it?'

'Yes,' sighed Angela. 'But poison is against my principles. And—this mandrake has a right to live, as much as anything else has. It's not its fault that it's out of place here. If I can't fight it on my own terms, I won't fight it at all.'

The frog beamed. Insofar as this is possible without lips and teeth.

'You have passed the test, Angela,' it said, in a changed voice. 'You have proved that you are sweet and gentle as well as efficient, hardworking and gifted in the art of transformation. Now, on full moon night, the time has come. If you kiss me, and wish, I will turn into a handsome prince. Then we can be married and your life will be complete.'

Angela hesitated, and took a step backwards. The frog's announcement had come as quite a shock, and offered, besides, much food for thought.

'Ah, Angela,' murmured the frog. 'Don't be afraid to follow your heart. Don't turn your back on the chance of a full, rich life. Don't choose the path of barrenness, disappointment and bitterness.'

Angela nodded. 'When you put it like that . . .' she said.

So she stepped forward, narrowly avoiding crushing the frog, wished, and kissed the mandrake. In the blink of an eye, the mandrake had changed into a magnificent white magnolia in full bloom.

The frog muttered something about there being lots of pebbles on the beach and hopped away to find a woman more appreciative of his potential. He'd had his eye on Mrs Knight, the widow three doors up, for some time, anyway.

And Angela, freed from both the mandrake and her last, lingering doubts about her choice of lifestyle, lived happily ever after.